The Mirrorman

by Brian Way

Edited with notes by Margaret Faulkes

THE MIRRORMAN was first published by Theatre Centre, Ltd., London, England in 1964. It was written and directed by the author for presentation to children in schools and was toured throughout the British Isles for a year. The script was first published by Young Audience Scripts, Edmonton, Canada.

Baker's Plays
7611 Sunset Blvd.
Los Angeles, CA 90042
bakersplays.com

THE MIRRORMAN

Characters (in order of appearance):
TOYMAN
MIRRORMAN, his reflection
BEAUTY, a doll-that-can-walk-and-talk
WITCH

The scene throughout is the Toyman's workshop.

Type of Participation: Whole audience.

Running time: 50 minutes.

PRODUCTION NOTES

AUDIENCE PARTICIPATION: Intimate staging is a necessary condition for the best results in audience participation: the whole room becomes the 'theatre', the actors and audience sharing the same space and the same experiences. The closer the children are to the action, the more genuine their involvement; intimacy thus determines a limited audience - the smaller the better.

CHILDREN OF THIS AGE RANGE (5-8 years) are not yet 'conditioned' to adult theatre behavior; their spontaneous response is triggered by emotional and physical reactions to the characters and action in the play. The genuine quality of such reaction is directly related to the genuine quality of the acting. Caricatures, unbelievable behavior or phony emotions will be recognized by the young audience for what they are.

INTEGRATED PARTICIPATION involving **IMPROVISATIONS:** The play is intended as an experience of live theatre for children, and as such is structured with the characters and their story in mind. Participation is integrated in that action of the play could not continue if the audience did not help the characters at key moments. At such moments, improvisation is required of the characters and of the audience. The structure of the play controls these moments and at other times participation should neither be sought nor encouraged other than through normal sympathetic contact between actor and audience.

CREATIVE DRAMA: While links with educational concepts in Creative Drama are inherent, the play is not intended as an opportunity for spontaneous, uncontrolled creative drama activities to develop. These are best encouraged after the play has ended. Nevertheless, center staging, fluid action and participation relate directly to the kind of creative drama encouraged with elementary age group children, and the directors are referred to the author's text on drama in education: DEVELOPMENT THROUGH DRAMA by Brian Way.

NOTES ON PARTICIPATION ARE GIVEN AT THE END OF THE PLAY.

STAGING THE PLAY

The following notes pertain to the original production of the play which was directed by the author. They are intended as information.

SETTING: A hall/gymnasium using an oval acting area with the audience seated on the floor. Note: the acting area, entrances etc. may be indicated by masking tape or chalk.

LIGHTING: It has been well established that children of this age range have no need of lighting; indeed, lighting can provide a barrier and, if changes occur, interrupt concentration. Daylight, or the normal overhead lighting is all that is necessary.

COSTUMES: Children of this age enjoy strong, primary colors. Costumes should be simple and believable. "Cartoon" clothes imply caricatures. In the original production, a "timeless" quality was effected:

TOYMAN and MIRRORMAN: dark brown breeches, stockings, shoes; gold colored shirt, red neckerchief; grey wig and steel-rimmed reading glasses.

BEAUTY: A two colored blue/pink denim dress, white knee socks.

WITCH: A dark green midi-length dress, with a border of orange lightning flashes; a close concept of witch rather than the traditional tall hat - hump backed - black robed type.

OLD LADY (Witch): A hat and large shawl. Note: this did not completely cover her witch's costume.

EDITOR'S NOTE: The characters of TOYMAN and MIRRORMAN first appeared in a play entitled "The Storytellers" by Brian Way. Reference to their original meeting was made by Mirrorman and Toyman in the first version of The Mirrorman but proved to be confusing for actors/audience and is omitted in this edition of the play.

THE MIRRORMAN

We are in the Toyman's workshop at one end of which is a full-length mirror; suddenly the Toyman runs in, bubbling with delight and excitement, calling to us, the audience, as he enters.

TOYMAN — Listen, everybody, I've done it, I've done it, I'VE DONE IT! I've finished making the most beautiful doll I've ever seen. And d'you know what? She can walk - yes, she can; she can really walk. And she can talk. Think how wonderful that is - she can actually talk! And do you know what I've called her? Do you? (1)* No, of course you don't know. How can you when I haven't told you yet? Well, I'll tell you now. I've called her - Beauty. Beauty. Isn't that a beautiful name for a beautiful doll? Beauty. Ooooh, but you must see Beauty walk. It really is amazing how she does it. All she has to do is listen carefully until she hears this: POM-POM-POM-POM-POM-POM-POM- and at once she starts walking. Would you like to see her do it? Would you? All right, then. But will you help me with the Pom-pom-pom-pom-pom-pom-pom? Will you? All right. Let's try it. (2)

With the Pom-pom-pom-pom-pom-pom-poms, Beauty enters, walking to the beat of the voices, behind the audience and into the acting area. Toyman's voice brings the poms to a stop.

TOYMAN — There - you see. Isn't it wonderful? Thank you for helping with the poms. It makes me a bit hoarse if I have to do it on my own all the time. Now listen - just you listen to this. *(He turns all his concentration on Beauty.)* Hello, Beauty. *(No reaction so he tries again.)* Hello, Beauty. *(She turns her head and smiles at him.)* Hello.

Beauty, because she is a doll, speaks rather stiffly at first...

BEAUTY — Hel-lo.

TOYMAN — *(Gently)* Again. *(No reaction.)* Again.

BEAUTY — A-gain.

TOYMAN — *(Warmly amused and patient.)* No, no, no, no, not "again". Say "hello" again.

BEAUTY — Hel-lo a-gain.

TOYMAN — *(Chuckling both at the mistake and the triumph.)* Well, well, yes, yes - yes, I suppose that is what I asked you to say. *(To audience)* It's very difficult for her, isn't it? But she's doing well. Jolly well, I think. Oooooh, Beauty. You can say hello to all my friends. Go on - they're delighted to meet you.

BEAUTY — Hel-lo - to - all - my - friends.

TOYMAN — Well done, well done, Beauty. *(To audience)* She really is learning very fast. Soon she'll be able to talk all on her own - think how exciting that'll be. I know - let's try walking once more: then you can sit

Numbers in parentheses refer to participation notes at the end of the play.

down and have a rest over here while I get ready. Come on - let's try.(3) Pom-pom-pom-pom-pom-pom-pom-pom-pom-pom. *(Beauty stops in front of the hinged box.)* Now, all we need is an Ooooooff Plonk and she'll be able to sit down. Let's try it (4) OOOOOoofff Plonk. *(And Beauty sits)* There we are. See - it does work. All right, Beauty, my beauty, you sit there and have a rest and think about more words while I get tidied up. I shan't be long.

BEAUTY — Don't - be - long.

TOYMAN — No, no, no, no. I shan't be long. All right now?

BEAUTY — All - right - now. Thank-you.

TOYMAN — *(Tickled all over with delight-to audience)* Isn't she beautiful? Oooh - my book. I must get my book. I won't be a moment.

And he rushes off to get his book.

BEAUTY — *(To audience)* Where - has - he - gone?

Answers of varying kinds may come (5) in which case she can discuss the matter until the Toyman returns with his book. It is an enormous book with a big label on it saying: INSTRUCTIONS — WHO? WHEN? WHAT?

TOYMAN — Here we are.

BEAUTY — Hel-lo. Where - have - you - been?

TOYMAN — I've been to get my book. Oh, now, come on Beauty, you're supposed to be having a rest. Now off you go to sleep. Off to sleep. That's it, fast asleep...fast asleep.

And she goes to sleep.

TOYMAN — She needs the rest, you know. Too much excitement - well, you know. Now, where are we? (6) Oh, yes, the book. Of course, of course.

For all his years experience the Toyman has never ever fully mastered the arts and needs of bookmanship; He doesn't really like it and, though he appreciates the basic needs, he's always glad to forget about it. Over the years, this has brought about a kind of absent-mindedness every time he has anything to do with the book. So now he peers at its front cover, almost as though he were reminding himself about it.

TOYMAN — The book. *(Reading)* INSTRUCTIONS; WHO? WHAT? WHEN? *(To Audience)* It has to be, you know. If I didn't have this book I should get in such a muddle. I'd make all the wrong things and send them to the wrong people at the wrong time and the wrong address - oh, it really would be just about as higgledy as piggledy could get. But this gets it all sorted out. It tells me exactly **what** to make, **who** to make it for, and **when** I promised it would be ready by. So let's see who I made Beauty for, then I'll know where to take her. *(Looking away from the book* *with a moment of sadness)* Not that I want to take her anywhere. Not really. I'm so thrilled about her that I'd like to keep her all to myself. Still. *(Cheering up again)* No point in thinking like that. I wouldn't be a very good toymaker if I kept all the toys just to myself. So, let's see. *(Reading)* "Doll that goes ma-ma", "Doll that stands on one leg", "Doll that has hiccoughs" *(Chuckling)* - that was a very tricky one to make, I can tell you - *(Reading again)* "Doll that giggles", - ah, here we are - "Doll that walks and talks" - page ten. Let's see now. Page 10. (7) Page 6 - 7 - 8 - 9 - 10. *(Looking down the page)* Doll that can walk - and - talk. Here it is. What! What's this? No name!! Oh dear, what have I done now? No name! No - ah! Now I remember. I was standing in the shop when in walks this old lady. *(He acts both roles as if it were in the present)* "Good morning" says she. "Good morning" says I. "Could I", says she, "have a doll that walks and talks?" "Well," says I, "I'm afraid you can't because I haven't made one." "Well," says she, "would you please make one for me. I'll call for it on - *(And the Toyman gives whatever is today's date)*". "What name?" says I. And by the time I've found my book she's gone. Disappeared altogether. Just like that. Poof! Gone! Hey - just a minute - what was that date again? (8) *(He repeats today's date)*. Why - that's today! Hooo - what good luck I've finished it in time. Well, I'd better get tidied up in case she comes. No good looking untidy when a customer arrives.

He goes to the mirror and, as he reaches it, so too does the Mirrorman who, of course, is very similar to the Toyman in such externals as clothes and so on. He is not so, however, in temperament (nor necessarily very exactly so in physique); he can be and often is a cantankerous old so and so, but at the same time is extremely likeable so that we, the audience, are anxious and willing to help him when he needs our help. As the Toyman arrives at the mirror he is carrying his big book, and the Mirrorman is carrying a similar book labelled in the same manner. Straightway the Toyman puts down his book on the box which supports the mirror. Since the Mirrorman is his reflection he does exactly the same and proceeds to make identical movements at the identical moment as Toyman begins to tidy himself up, humming and chatting to himself as he does so.

TOYMAN — Oh, I don't think I look so bad. No worse than usual, anyway. Tidy the eyebrows . . . that's it . . . smooth down the hair . . . there and there . . . and - oh dear! This mirror does get dirty; doesn't seem to make any difference how often I clean it - the next second it's all dirty again. Never mind. Do it again. *(He takes a dusting cloth from his pocket, with which he now cleans the mirror)* . . . . . . There. That's better. *(He shakes the dust away)* Much better. For a little while anyway. Oh dear! I'm going to sneeze . . . ah - ah-ah-ah-ah-ah-tishoo. *(The Mirrorman sneezes too)* . . . ah-ah-ah-ah-ah-ah-ah-ah-tishoo . . . ah-ah-ah-ah - ah *(And he just manages to stop the third sneeze - but the Mirrorman does sneeze. Toyman is astonished and swings round to look at him.*

then - to audience) That's funny! Did he sneeze when I didn't? (9) I think he did, you know. *(He looks again but all seems well.)* I wonder what he's up to? I'll soon find out.

He begins a sequence of movements, some of them slow and calculated, some fast and sudden. The Mirrorman keeps exactly with him at first. Then Toyman crouches down behind his book, ready to bob up, but before he does, Mirrorman calls out from behind his book-

MIRROR — Help!

Toyman is astonished and remains very still. Then slowly and a little fearfully peers over the top of his book - Mirrorman does the same.

TOYMAN — Oh dear, I don't like this a bit.

And rather involuntarily, prompted more by fear than cunning, he begins a sequence of very quick and agile movements until the Mirrorman can't stand it any more.

MIRROR — Stop, stop, stop, stop, STOP.

Toyman drops to the floor in an astonished heap.

TOYMAN — Well, I never did.

MIRROR — No, and I never did neither. Bobbing up and down, backwards and forwards . . .

TOYMAN — Well, you see -

MIRROR — From side to side round and round . .

TOYMAN — Well, it's -

MIRROR — Once and for all will you kindly note I am not a jack-in-the-box.

TOYMAN — But I didn't realize. Otherwise -

MIRROR — Did you or did you not hear me call "Help"?

TOYMAN — Oh, so it was you.

MIRROR — Of course it was me, silly. Who else could it have been?

TOYMAN — That's what I wondered.

MIRROR — I've been trying to attract your attention for days.

TOYMAN — Have you? I didn't know.

MIRROR — Of course you didn't know. You wouldn't pay any attention. Didn't matter what I did - tap on the mirror, breathe on it and make my side all cloudy - even throw dust on it - you take no notice at all.

TOYMAN — When have you done all those things?

MIRROR — All sorts of times - when you've been wandering about the shop, and when you've been writing in your book - even when you've been having a snooze. And all you do is mutter to yourself "that's funny - do I hear noises?" and then take no more notice.

TOYMAN — But you never said anything when I was standing in front of the mirror.

MIRROR — Of course I didn't silly. I'm not allowed to. It's one of the rules. *(Opening up his book)* It says so here - where are we? Ah - here we are. Rule 7: "In front of the mirror you must only do and say what the other person does and says." See! That's rule 7.

TOYMAN — Then are you breaking the rule now?

MIRROR — No, of course not, silly. Otherwise I wouldn't do it. Listen - there's another rule about breaking the rule - *(He looks it up because he is becoming a bit flustered himself about the logic of all this)* - it's all quite clear really. Here, listen. "This rule can only be broken if and when you really need help." See?

TOYMAN — Yes, I see. I'm sorry.

MIRROR — Good, that's settled. Now -

TOYMAN — But what sort of help do you need?

MIRROR — Time enough to tell you that when I've come through the mirror.

TOYMAN — Are - are you going to come through the mirror?

MIRROR — Of course I am, silly. You can't be much help if you're in that room and I'm in this, can you?

TOYMAN — No, I suppose not.

MIRROR — Come on, then, I'm ready. *(He stands with his hands flat against the mirror. Pause.)* Come on then.

TOYMAN — What?

MIRROR — *(Becoming rather cantakerous)* What do you mean "what"?

TOYMAN — Well - er - what?

MIRROR — I can't just wander through the mirror like water down a drain. It's very difficult business and I have to have help with it.

TOYMAN — Yes, but what do you want me to do?

MIRROR — Well, you have to - you have to keep on and on - no. It's not that. That's for something else. Oh dear - you've got me all muddled. Wait a minute. *(He opens his book)* Let's see. *(Reading)* "Instructions - for getting through mirrors. Page one thousand two hundred and thirty-four". We'd better get it right. It's very difficult you know. Here we are -

page one two three four. "Instructions for getting through mirrors: Take more than 100 *(Or whatever number is in the audience)* voices and make them go Hummmmmmmmmmmmm".

TOYMAN — So we all help with the hum.

MIRROR — If there are more than 100 of you - yes please.

TOYMAN — Oh, I'm sure we're more than a hundred, aren't we? (10) Good. Now, you get ready and -

MIRROR — *(Impatiently)* I **am** ready.

TOYMAN — All right, all right, all right. there's no need to be cross.

MIRROR — I am not cross - I am urgent.

TOYMAN — *(A bit irritated himself)* All right then.

MIRROR — All right, I'm ready.

TOYMAN — Now - hummmmmmmmmmmmmmmmm (11).

As we all hum, the Mirrorman slowly oozes his way through the mirror. Note - he has emphasized that this is a difficult business. Beauty wakes up with the hum.

TOYMAN — There! You've done it. you've done it.

MIRROR — *(Pleased)* Of course I've done it. *(To audience)* Thanks very much.

Suddenly Mirrorman remembers something terribly important -

MIRROR — *(With consternation)* Oh no! No, No!

TOYMAN — What's the matter?

MIRROR — I've forgotten the most important thing of all - my book! I've forgotten my book. I must go back for it! Oh, dear, I hope I'm not too late. Ohhh - LOOK!!! -

And we all look where he is pointing - through the mirror. . .and there is the Witch moving slowly and stealthily towards where he left his book.

MIRROR — Oh no, no, no. Help me everybody. Quickly.

TOYMAN — What do we do?

MIRROR — Wish. Wish with all your might that she doesn't reach the book. Quickly - wish - wish . . . (12)

We all wish with all our might - and as the influence of the wish reaches her, the Witch finds it more and more difficult to move towards the book, struggle as she may to do so. Her fingers nearly reach it...

MIRROR — Harder - wish harder - wish - wish -

*And as we wish harder, so we slowly drive the Witch away from the
book, still reaching out towards it . . . till suddenly she gives up and
turns and runs away.*

MIRROR — Oh, gosh, that was a near thing. Thanks everyone. Now,
there's no time to lose. Help me back through the mirror so that I can
fetch it.

TOYMAN — Are you ready?

MIRROR — *(Standing with his hands flat against the mirror)* Yes, yes,
I'm ready.

TOYMAN — Now - the hum (13)

*Again we all hum - and the Mirrorman goes back through the mirror,
picks up his book, turns and with the hum comes back through -
just in time -*

TOYMAN — Look out!

*Mirrorman leaps down from the mirror box just as the Witch again
appears - she goes swiftly to where the book was - searches distractedly
for it - can't find it and suddenly looks up through the mirror . . .*

WITCH — It will soon be mine - it will soon be mine -

She turns and disappears swiftly.

BEAUTY — I - don't - like - her - one - little - bit.

MIRROR — Who said that?

TOYMAN — Oh! This is my new doll. Beauty. I've just finished making
her and . . .

BEAUTY — How - do - you - do?

MIRROR — Ah, yes, I've watched you making her. How do you do? Very
clever of you.

TOYMAN — Watched me?

MIRROR — Of course I've watched you. When I've not been busy somewhere else.

TOYMAN — Somewhere else? Do you mean you go to other places besides
here?

MIRROR — Of course I do, silly. I cover the whole of this block. That's
why I have to take the book wherever I go. You can't be too careful.
If I let it out of my sight for one minute, anything might happen.

TOYMAN — But your book's exactly like my book. *(He fetches his own)*

MIRROR — Naturally - when I'm working with you. But only on the
outside even then. The inside's quite different.

TOYMAN — Really?

MIRROR — Of course. It has all my spells and my magic and my instructions in it. That's why the Witch wants to get it. But we're going to stop her - we've got to stop her. If we don't stop her -

TOYMAN — So that's what you were calling help about.

MIRROR — What else? I tell you if we don't stop her, then - then -

TOYMAN — Then what?

MIRROR — I don't know "then what". But it'll be terrible, I tell you, terrible -

TOYMAN — All right, all right - stop going on about it. You'll give us the creeps. We'll all help you, but it'll have to wait a bit.

MIRROR — But we can't wait.

TOYMAN — We'll have to wait.

MIRROR — No, no, NO.

TOYMAN — Yes, yes, YES.

MIRROR — Why?

TOYMAN — Because - well, for the very simple reason that I have my work to do.

MIRROR — You can take a day off.

TOYMAN — Yes, but not today. I have a customer coming today - any minute in fact.

MIRROR — Who?

TOYMAN — I - I don't know her name. But she's coming in to collect Beauty, and we'll have to wait for her.

BEAUTY — I don't mind waiting till tommorrow. *(Her speech becomes more fluent from now on, retaining a staccato quality.)*

TOYMAN — That's very kind of you Beauty. But it's out of the question. I never let a customer down once I've given my promise.

BEAUTY — Listen!

As we all listen we hear knocking in the shop outside.

MIRROR — Maybe that's your customer now. I hope so - then we can get on with things.

BEAUTY — Oh, but please, I don't want to go yet. I want to stay and help.

TOYMAN — Well, you may have to go, Beauty.

BEAUTY — But -

TOYMAN — I'm sorry, but that's the arrangement. Now, you two wait here and I'll go and see who it is.

There is more knocking as the Toyman goes. He leaves his book on a box opposite Beauty. Mirrorman walks up and down partly with impatience, partly thinking up what to do next. Beauty watches him for a while.

BEAUTY — *(Half whispering)* Mr. Mirrorman. *(No answer - so a bit louder)* Mr. Mirrorman!

MIRROR — Well?

BEAUTY — Sorry. Were - you - thinking?

MIRROR — I was. But never mind.

BEAUTY — Why don't you put your book in this box? It'll be safe there.

MIRROR — Which box? This one? *(Going to the one where the Toyman left his book)*

BEAUTY — The one I'm sitting on. It's only got clothes in it.

MIRROR — I don't like to let the book out of my sight.

BEAUTY — Well, it won't be really, will it? I mean - you'll know where it is but no one else will; especially if you cover it up with the clothes. If you hold it in your hand than everyone can see it.

MIRROR — *(After a moment's thought)* Good idea. Up you get.

BEAUTY — I can't on my own. You all have to go "Plonk Oooofff".

MIRROR — Plonk Ooooff?

BEAUTY — Yes. It's Ooooff Plonk for sitting and Plonk Ooooff for standing.

MIRROR — Plonk Ooooff. All right.

BEAUTY — Hadn't we better hurry?

ALL — Plonk Ooooooooffffff.

Beauty gets up and the Mirrorman quickly puts his book into the box which has a hinged top.

BEAUTY — Cover it well with the clothes.

MIRROR — There. That's it.

BEAUTY — Now an Ooooff Plonk if you please.

ALL — Oooofff Plonk.

And Beauty sits.

BEAUTY — I'm sure it'll be safe there.

MIRROR — Thank you, Beauty.

Toyman returns with an Old Lady, talking as he enters.

TOYMAN — Oh, yes, indeed she can walk. She walks very well; all she needs is a pom-pom-pom to help her. And she stands with a Plonk Ooooofff and sits with an Oooofff Plonk. I think you'll find her very satisfactory. *(As they arrive in the area he stops with another thought)* Oh! I nearly forgot. I hope you won't mind, but I've given her a name. I've called her "Beauty".

OLD LADY — A delightful name. And very suitable. Hello, Beauty. How-do-you-do? I understand you can talk. (15)

BEAUTY — Yes, I can talk. How-do-you-do?

OLD LADY — And you're going to come with me.

BEAUTY — Am I?

She sounds definitely reluctant, so the Toyman cuts in.

TOYMAN — Well - er - well, we must show the lady how you can walk. All right?

BEAUTY — All right. *(Quietly)* I suppose.

TOYMAN — Ready everyone? We must get her up first. Now -

We help her to get up with a plonk ooofff and then help her to walk with pom - pom - pom - pom; while the Toyman is absorbed with this and Beauty is absorbed doing it, the Mirrorman watches the old lady with suspicion as she surreptitiously looks around. Mirrorman sidles up to Toyman.

MIRROR — *(Hissing)* We must hurry with this.

TOYMAN — Shan't be long . . . pom-pom-pom-pom-POM-POM. *(To climax and stop)* Well done, Beauty.

Beauty has stopped in the middle of the area. The following is all in urgent whispers:

BEAUTY — I don't think I want to go with her. She doesn't smell right to me.

TOYMAN — Now, Beauty, you musn't be like that. I don't want you to go either, but then it's part of the arrangements.

MIRROR — Hurry, hurry.

BEAUTY — No, I won't go.

TOYMAN — But you must go.

MIRROR — Go or stay - please yourselves. But do get on with it.

They continue the argument in whispers. Meanwhile the old lady picks up Toyman's book and glides away with it. Either through audience warning (15) or seeing her themselves, Mirrorman and Toyman note her departure and give chase . . . but she gets away. The two men return.

TOYMAN — It's never happened to me before. Nobody has ever deceived me like that. Never, never, never.

BEAUTY — *(Still in the same place)* I told you she didn't smell right.

TOYMAN — And to think I nearly gave Beauty to her. Oh dear, oh dear, oh dear.

MIRROR — Thank goodness it was your book she got and not mine. (16)

TOYMAN — What do you mean "my book"?

MIRROR — Well, it was your book she stole. Thanks to Beauty I'd hidden mine in the box there -

TOYMAN — What? What? My book? Oh, this is terrible.

MIRROR — It would be more terrible still if she'd taken mine.

TOYMAN — So you may think. But that book's got all my Who, When, and Whats in it. Now I shall get all higgledy piggledy. . .

MIRROR — Wait a minute! I've just has a dreadful thought. She'll come back! As soon as she realizes she's got the wrong book, she'll come back again. Now do you see why it's so urgent we shouldn't wait for anything else?

TOYMAN — *(Very distressed)* Yes, yes. I do see. But what are we to do about it?

MIRROR — We'll be ready for her - that's what. Help me with some of these clothes and we'll take them into your shop.

TOYMAN — *(As they dig out the clothes)* Now, please be careful. These are clothes I need for some of the other dolls.

MIRROR — Don't worry about that. They'll be all right.

TOYMAN — *(As they begin to go)* What about Beauty?

MIRROR — Leave her here. We shan't be long. Come on -

BEAUTY — *(Calling after them)* Can't I sit down, please?

MIRROR — *(Calling back)* Soon, soon. There's no time to waste.

And with Toyman protesting, they go.

BEAUTY — *(To audience)* As they're so busy, would you all help me please? Thank you. Just some poms to get me over to the box and an Oooofff Plonk to sit me down. (17)

We all help to pom-pom-pom-pom her over to the hinged box and with an oooofff plonk she sits.

BEAUTY — Thank you very much. That's much better.

But she is no sooner settled than the Witch comes back - carrying the Toyman's book which she eventually sets down. (18)

WITCH — Now - you. Where is the real book?

BEAUTY — *(At her sauciest)* What real book?

WITCH — You know perfectly well what book I mean.

BEAUTY — Oh, go and write your own book. You're nothing but a - but - a bully.

WITCH — Tell me where it is - now.

BEAUTY — Shan't.

WITCH — Ah! So you do know where it is.

BEAUTY — *(Confused)* You're just trying to muddle me 'cos I'm not very good at talking.

WITCH — If you don't tell me where that book is you won't talk at all.

BEAUTY — Shan't.

WITCH — I'll give you up to three.

BEAUTY — I don't know what three is.

WITCH — One . . . (19)

BEAUTY — Shan't.

WITCH — Two . . .

BEAUTY — Shan't.

WITCH — Three . . .

BEAUTY — Sha . . .

But she doesn't get out the whole word, for at that moment the Witch, with a sound and a swift movement, puts a spell on her that makes it impossible for her to speak any more.

WITCH — There. I said I'd do it. Now perhaps you'll know better than to defy me. The moment you show me where the book is I'll take the spell off you. If you don't - then worse will follow.

Beauty makes defiant sounds while shaking her head.

WITCH — Now - where is it? *(Beauty is defiant.)* Just point to where it is and I'll do the rest. *(More defiant, so Witch wheedles:)* Now, I'm not asking very much - and as soon as I find it you shall have your speech back again. Think how lovely that will be. *(Even tougher defiance.)* Very well, you stupid girl. Once more I'll give you up to three - if you haven't shown me by then, I'll put another spell on you which will stop you from moving. *(More defiance)* One . . . two . . . three . . .

And the Witch puts another spell on her which freezes Beauty into stillness.

WITCH — There. Perhaps you'll know better than to defy me in the future. I'll find it myself.

She begins to search for it without success. Then she hears Toyman and Mirrorman approaching. She turns swiftly to Beauty and, using her hands, weaves a new spell over Beauty saying:

WITCH — If by chance they break my spell The first thing then that you will tell: Exactly where the book is hid. Calling loud and clear to me: "Witch - come here and you shall see!" That is what the spell does bid.

With a final swift movement confirming the new spell the Witch disappears. Mirrorman and Toyman return disguised as wizards. (Note: it is helpful if any headgear is carried and put on at the final moment of preparation for becoming wizards.)

TOYMAN — But are you sure it'll work?

MIRROR — Of course it'll work - just as long as we can get Beauty through the mirror.

TOYMAN — But how are we going to do that?

MIRROR — You'll see. *(He sniffs around)* Wait. Someone's been here. (20)

TOYMAN — Who?

MIRROR — I'm not sure. Possibly the Witch.

TOYMAN — *(To Beauty)* Has she been here Beauty? *(No answer)* Beauty - has the witch been back? *(No answer)*

MIRROR — There, what did I tell you?

TOYMAN — *(Urgently)* Beauty! Beauty!

MIRROR — It's no good talking to her - she's under a spell.

TOYMAN — But that's terrible! Beauty. Beauty can you hear me?

MIRROR — I don't think she can move either. Try a Plonk Oooofff.

Toyman tries a plonk ooooffff, but Beauty does not move.

TOYMAN — Oh, no, no she can't move. This is terrible. Oh, I shall get so angry in a minute.

MIRROR — Wait. Keep your anger for another time. We must find out what's happened.

TOYMAN — How?

MIRROR — By asking our frinds here - they'll know. *(To Audience)* you tell us what happened?

> *Mirrorman and Toyman turn to the audience to hear what happened (21). Mirrorman remains fairly calm whereas Toyman gets more and more distressed. Finally, Mirrorman calls to Toyman.*

MIRROR — Listen! (22) Now we know what happened. The first spell stopped Beauty from being able to speak. The second stopped her from being able to move. Well, we can get rid of those easily enough. But the third -

TOYMAN — *(Anxiously)* Yes?

MIRROR — Well - we'll worry about that in a minute. Help me to move Beauty onto this other box so that we can get at my book.

TOYMAN — *(As they are moving Beauty)* Careful with her -

MIRROR — I **am** being careful.

TOYMAN — Will the book really help?

MIRROR — If it doesn't I shall send it back - it's got pages on how to deal with witches so there ought to be something. We can't just stand here holding her. Put her down, man.

TOYMAN — Carefully, then - she's very delicate. There, that's it.

> *The moment she is down Mirrorman dashes to the box and gets his book out.*

TOYMAN — Oh dear, I do hope it can help.

MIRROR — *(Going through the pages)* Stop fussing, man.

TOYMAN — And what's the point of our dressing up as Wizards?

MIRROR — You'll see, you'll see. Give me time.

TOYMAN — Time? That's all very well -

MIRROR — Now, listen to me. Are you or are you not going to stop fussing? Because if you don't I'll start some spells, see. I'll turn you into a cabbage, I will.

TOYMAN — *(Getting angry)* There'd be more point if you turned the witch into a cabbage.

MIRROR — You can't turn a witch into a cabbage. Doesn't work. Now will you please leave this to me. Please.

TOYMAN — All right. *(He controls his impatience and anxiety with difficulty.)*

MIRROR — Ah - here we are: "Doll dust for taking off witches' spells".

He begins to read, with Toyman hovering anxiously. Finally, Mirror-man bangs the book shut. . .

MIRROR — No good. Can't be done.

TOYMAN — What d'you mean it can't be done?

MIRROR — Too difficult. Much too difficult.

TOYMAN — Nonsense. Absolute nonsense. It can't be **too** difficult.

MIRROR — Yes it is. Sorry!

TOYMAN — *(Exploding)* Well, I like that. You - you - you monster! You turn up here - disturbing all the arrangements - telling us how much you need help to look after your book. You get us all in trouble simply because we try to help, and then you dare - you dare to stand there telling me that something's too difficult. Well, let me tell you it isn't. If you won't do it, then we will. So give me your wretched book and we'll get on with it. See?

He tries to snatch the book, the Mirrorman is too quick for him and moves out of the way, highly delighted.

MIRROR — That's it. That's what we need - to be urgent and determined. Now - stand by.

TOYMAN — *(Flabbergasted)* Do you mean to say -

MIRROR — Never mind. The main thing is to get on with it. Now, I'm going to read out what we need and you must all help (23). Everybody - curl up as small as you can. *(He waits for them to do so)* Now, with the sound I make, grow into big apple trees. *(Using his hands banging on one of the boxes, he makes a sound which grows to a climax as they grow)* Now - a wind blows the trees and all the apples are blown to the ground . . . let's hear the wind. . . Right! And pick up the apples . . . and put them in your lap *(As they do this they will automatically sit down)*. Now - eat the apples and save the pits. . .throw the apple cores away as far as you can. Right! Now - grind the pits into powder and save it carefully. . .Wonderful! Wonderful! Now everything is ready to take off the spell.

TOYMAN — Wait a minute! What about that third spell?

MIRROR — I know, I know: the third spell means that the instant Beauty can speak she is going to call out to the Witch and tell her where the book is. Well, don't worry. Listen. *(He takes Toyman quietly to one side and tells him secretly)* Beauty still thinks the book is in that box. Well - we'll put it somewhere else!

TOYMAN — Yes, but what happens if the witch puts a spell on us - or another spell on Beauty.

MIRROR — We'll wish her away - like we did before.

TOYMAN — Do you think it'll work?

MIRROR — Of course it will - if it's powerful enough. Wait till I give the word. Now - let's release Beauty from the spell.

TOYMAN — The book first. Where are we going to put it?

MIRROR — Oh yes. We'll ask someone to look after it. *(He speaks to audience)* Will someone look after it for me? (24) Thank you, thank you - but please, PLEASE don't open it because if you do the magic will leak out of it. All right? *(To Toyman)* As soon as we've released Beauty, follow me and hide.

TOYMAN — Yes, yes. Oh, I do so hope -

MIRROR — You're fussing again.

TOYMAN — Sorry.

MIRROR — Now - everyone. Blow the powder towards Beauty - Now!

As the powder is blown, Beauty is released from the spell to the growing excitement of Toyman. Gradually she is able to move a little, flexing her rather stiff joints - and then she is fully free. At once she calls out loud and clear as Mirrorman rushes away followed by Toyman. They hide among the audience.

BEAUTY — *(Calling)* Witch, Witch the spell is clear - Quickly come - the book is here!

At once, with a cry of triumph the Witch appears.

WITCH — Where is it? Where is the book?

BEAUTY — *(Despite herself)* It's in - that box, over there.

WITCH — *(Triumphantly)* That box over there!

At once she rushes to the box and begins feverishly to search for it. She realizes the book is not in the box. . . She turns to Beauty.

WITCH — It isn't here. It isn't here. You've tricked me. Where is it?

BEAUTY — But it was in the box. Truly it was.

WITCH — Truly. . . *(She realizes Mirrorman has tricked her and senses danger)* Where are they? Where are the Mirrorman and Toyman?

BEAUTY — I - I don't know.

WITCH — Of course you know. Tell me at once.

BEAUTY — Really I don't. They hid somewhere - oh! *(She is horrified that she has given them away)* No - no -

WITCH — So, they're hidden somewhere. They think they can trick me. Well, they'll have to learn that they can't. And I'll start with another spell on you, Beauty - and this will be a spell they won't be able to break. I'll give you up to three to tell me where they are.

BEAUTY — No - please - no!

The Witch starts slowly to approach her, counting as she moves.

WITCH — One. . .

MIRROR — Wish - wish - wish - (25)

And we all wish and slowly stop the Witch from getting near enough to Beauty to make the spell - suddenly she gives up and rushes away, crying aloud. . .

WITCH — I shall be back - I shall be back - and I shall win.

She disappears and immediately Toyman and Mirrorman come out of hiding.

TOYMAN — We should have pounced on her and tied her up.

MIRROR — That would be no good. She's cleverer than you think.

TOYMAN — Are you all right, Beauty?

BEAUTY — Yes, I'm all right. But I'm sorry I told her you were hiding.

TOYMAN — Don't worry about that -

MIRROR — She would have found out for herself any minute.

TOYMAN — Well, what do we do now?

MIRROR — Use our disguises.

TOYMAN — You mean we're going to be Wizards?

MIRROR — Yes. If a Witch meets a Wizard, then she has to do what he says - and what we shall tell her to do will get rid of her from this place for ever!

TOYMAN — *(Horrified at his thought)* You mean we're going to - kill her?

BEAUTY — Oh dear, I don't like that idea.

MIRROR — No. It would need more than **us** to kill a witch. No - we are simply going to make certain she never comes near your shop again.

TOYMAN — But how?

MIRROR — We're going to make her look into - and **touch** - that mirror.

TOYMAN — The mirror?

MIRROR — Witches are afraid of mirrors. If they see themselves in a mirror, within a few hours they turn into stone. They are frightened even to touch one - and if ever they do, then never again do they go near that place. So - we are going to make her touch - and if possible look into - that mirror.

TOYMAN — How?

MIRROR — We'll use her own greed. Beauty, you must help us with this.

TOYMAN — Don't you think Beauty's had enough?

MIRROR — I think we've all had enough. Kindly don't interfere.

BEAUTY — I'll help any way I can.

MIRROR — Then, you're going to go through the mirror - and you're going to take my book with you. *(To Toyman)* Quickly fetch it.

> *TOYMAN retrieves the book from whoever has it.*

MIRROR — Good. Now, get her up and walk her over to the mirror. We'll all help.

> *With a plonk ooooofff and the necessary poms Beauty arrives at the mirror.*

MIRROR — Now, Beauty, put your hands flat on the mirror. *(She does so)* In a moment, we are going to hum so that you can get through the mirror. Just as you're through stretch out one hand behind you and take the book from me. Then jump down and hide on the other side. Understand?

BEAUTY — I understand.

MIRROR — Are you ready?

TOYMAN — Oh dear, I don't like this at all.

MIRROR — Stop fussing. Beauty - are you ready?

BEAUTY — Yes - yes, I'm ready.

MIRROR — Then - the hum.

> *And with the hum, Beauty oozes her way through the mirror. As she gets through she stretches back one hand and the Mirrorman pushes the book into it. Beauty goes right through then jumps down and hides.*

MIRROR — Good. Good.

TOYMAN — Will she be all right?

MIRROR — I hope so. I hope so.

TOYMAN — *(More alarmed than ever)* You mean she might not be?

MIRROR — I mean you never can tell with witches. But I think she will be. Now, we must make a spell to bring the Witch back here.

TOYMAN — You're going to **make** her come back?!

MIRROR — Naturally.

TOYMAN — But, but, but -

MIRROR — Are you afraid?

TOYMAN — Well - Well - *(Defiantly)* as a matter of fact - yes, I am. I'm not used to such goings on. . .

MIRROR — Well, don't worry. It'll soon be over. Now - everyone help me to the spell. (26)

Mirrorman leads the movement and words with Toyman following. The words and movements must convey great solemnity and power.

MIRROR — Fingers! *(He extends his hands and fingers, we do the same and then join him with magic words:)* Eeba, Eeba, Eeba Eeeeeb. Arms! *(He weaves patterns with his arms as he speaks the magic words:)* Aaba, Aaba, Aaba, Aaaaab. Whole self! *(He used his whole body as he speaks:)* Ooba, Ooba, Ooba, Oooooob. *(Strongly)* EEB! AAB! OOB!

Silence. Mirrorman and Toyman are very still.

MIRROR — It's working - it's working. She'll be here in about a minute. *(He goes quickly and crouches by the mirror)* Beauty - can you hear me?

BEAUTY — *(Out of sight)* Yes I can hear you.

MIRROR — The Witch will be here soon. Now - when you hear me say to her: "Look - look in the mirror" push the book up so that she can see it Understand?

BEAUTY — Yes - yes.

MIRROR — Good.

TOYMAN — *(He is anxious and nervous)* What do I do?

MIRROR — You, my friend, are a Wizard. So too am I. Between us, we are going to **make** the Witch look in the mirror. Remember - as long as she thinks you're a Wizard she'll be more afraid of you than you are of her. But don't let her suspect for a moment. Just do what I do. Listen! Here she comes. *(Solemnly)* We must welcome her.

NOTE: The Toyman is dreadfully afraid but anxious to do the right thing. Throughout the scene he makes a serious attempt to follow the Mirrorman's example, although occasionally making a slip which the Mirrorman tries to cover up. The Mirrorman throughout the whole scene is very serious. This is the climax of the play and the atmosphere should be one of intense effort on his part to bring about the downfall of the witch. There should be no attempt to encourage participation in this scene (27). Focus of attention should be entirely on the Witch. The Mirrorman takes up a solemn pose as the Witch appears in the aisle. . .she is slightly hesitant. . .

WITCH — What Wizard is it beckons me?

MIRROR — We beckon, Witch. Come in.

WITCH — Prove to me who you are.

MIRROR — You heard our calls?

WITCH — I heard - and I obeyed!

MIRROR — That is proof enough. Come in.

WITCH — *(Suspicious but moving a little nearer)* No - I require further proof.

MIRROR — What proof?

WITCH — *(To Toyman)* You - turn yourself into a toad.

TOYMAN — *(Aghast, fearful, indignant)* A what?

WITCH — A toad. Turn yourself into a toad.

TOYMAN — I'll do nothing of the sort!

WITCH — Then I will not come in. This may be a trick.

MIRROR — Our brother Wizard here is new to the brotherhood. But not so new that he can be caught by **your** trick. He knows as I do that witches **eat** toads - so you can hardly blame him for refusing. What would you say if I asked you to turn into - fire?

WITCH — I should refuse.

MIRROR — Exactly. Perhaps we can offer other proof.

TOYMAN — *(Barely audible)* Oh, I do hope so.

WITCH — What proof?

MIRROR — We know you have been to this place before.

WITCH — So?

MIRROR — We have come to help you - to help you - find the book.

WITCH — *(Eagerly)* You know where it is?

MIRROR — We do.

TOYMAN — *(Trying to be defiant)* Yes, we know exactly where it is, and you'll be luckier than you deserve if you get it. We - we -

MIRROR — *(Covering up but withering Toyman with a look)* What our brother means is that we were naturally tempted to take the book ourselves.

WITCH — And why haven't you?

MIRROR — Because - *(As he hesitates, Toyman tries to come to the rescue)*

TOYMAN — Because we have plans of our own!

WITCH — *(Sharply)* Plans? What plans?

MIRROR — Our brother means that one good turn deserves another. If we help you with the Book, perhaps one day you will help us.

WITCH — *(Still suspicious)* Perhaps!

TOYMAN — *(Working at his image)* Perhaps!

WITCH — Very well. I will come in. *(She does so)* Now - where is the book?

MIRROR — Look - look in the mirror -

At once Beauty pushes the book up behind the mirror.

WITCH — *(Alarmed)* No, no. You cannot ask me to look in the mirror. *(And she turns away from it)*

MIRROR — *(Urgently)* But you must. You must look. Look!

TOYMAN — *(Equally urgent)* Look in the mirror -

MIRROR — Look in the mirror -

WITCH — No, no -

MIRROR — You must -

TOYMAN — You must -

WITCH — *(Fighting with her own greed)* I cannot look in a mirror -

MIRROR — But the book you need so much is resting there -

TOYMAN — All you need from the whole of life is resting there.

MIRROR — Look -

TOYMAN — Look -

BOTH — Look - look in the mirror -

With a cry the Witch turns - goes halfway to the mirror and looks -

BOTH — See - see - the book - the book!

WITCH — *(Almost entranced by the sight)* The book! The book! The one thing I've wanted for years - the one thing that would give me power over the world beyond mirrors - that would make me the most powerful witch that ever lived.

MIRROR — Go and fetch it -

TOYMAN — Yes, go and fetch it - fetch it -

MIRROR — Fetch the book -

TOYMAN — Fetch the book -

MIRROR — Fetch the book -

Slowly, hypnotically, the Witch begins to move towards the mirror -

MIRROR — Think of the power -

TOYMAN — Think of the power -

BOTH — Power - power - power -

WITCH — Power- power - power - power - power - power -

And she is almost at the mirror: Mirrorman suddenly calls out:

MIRROR — Plonk Oooofff - Plonk Oooffff

Beauty automatically bobs up with the book and as the Witch dashes forward to catch it:

WITCH — Give it me - give it me - give it me -

MIRROR — *(Calling out strongly)* Laugh, Beauty - laugh everybody - laugh - laugh - laugh

As the laughter comes at the Witch it maddens her and she makes furious grasp at the book - and touches the mirror. She screams and still screaming turns and runs until she disappears. Toyman starts to run after her but Mirrorman stops him.

MIRROR — Leave her. Leave her. She'll never come back. (28)

TOYMAN — Gosh, I hope not. I couldn't go through all that again. Gosh, I was scared. And when she told me to turn myself into a toad - well I nearly dropped on the spot.

MIRROR — I must say that one foxed me a bit too. Never mind. *(He claps him on the shoulder.)* We did very well.

And highly pleased with themselves, they shake hands. Suddenly, Toyman remembers -

TOYMAN — Beauty! *(Runs to the mirror)* Beauty, are you all right?

BEAUTY — I'm fine thank you. Has she gone?

TOYMAN — Yes. She's gone forever.

BEAUTY — Oh, good. Then I can come back now.

TOYMAN — Yes, you can come back. Ready with the hum -

MIRROR — Wait! Wait. Let me go back first - if you don't mind.

TOYMAN — I don't mind a bit - but what's the hurry?

MIRROR — No real hurry - but I ought to get back to work - and there's a special thing I'd like to do - don't ask me what. You'll see. I'm ready for the hum now.

We all hum and he goes back through the mirror. (The Toyman keeping well back from it.) When he is through, the Mirrorman takes his

book back from Beauty with a dignified and courteous bow, but without a word. Toyman watches curiously. Mirrorman turns a few pages - reads - touches Beauty silently mouthing some words as he does so. Then -

MIRROR — Now Beauty, put your hands flat on the mirror. *(She does so.)* *(He nods to Toyman.)*

TOYMAN — Now the Hum.

Beauty comes back through the mirror. Toyman helps her down.

TOYMAN — Well done, Beauty, well done. And you won't have to leave me after all now that the witch has gone. *(He turns to the mirror)* Isn't that so, Mr. Mirrorman?

But Mirrorman has become a reflection again and merely does what the Toyman does.

TOYMAN — Oh - oh, I see. Well - never mind. Thanks for helping.

The last words are said very clearly by the Mirrorman at the same time - and then the Toyman backs slowly away, waving as does the Mirrorman AS HE GOES. Beauty suddenly draws our attention. . .

BEAUTY — Please - please - I feel very strange!

TOYMAN — *(Anxiously)* What sort of strange?

BEAUTY — I don't feel stiff any more. No - look! All my joints can move on their own - oh! - *(And she begins to walk, jump, sit, etc.)* Look! I shan't need any more Poms nor any more Plonk Oooofffs or Oooofff Plonks. Look! I can do it all on my own.

TOYMAN — But that't wonderful. What ever has happened?

BEAUTY — **He** did it! That's it! He did it when he touched me and whispered something. How kind of him.

TOYMAN — He's a **nice** man! I hope we see him again.

BEAUTY — Why of course we will - every time you look in the mirror!

TOYMAN — Of course! *(There is a pause and they both look at the mirror.)* Well - I suppose I'd better get back to work.

BEAUTY — Let me help you. There must be something I can do.

TOYMAN — *(Delighted)* Well, you could look after my book for me - to stop me from getting all higgledy piggledy you know. *(They begin to go.)* And there's all the clothes for the dolls. Come on, then, let's start right away. *(He stops.)* Oh - just a minute. *(To us)* Thanks very much for helping. See you again some day. Goodbye! *(And off they go.)*

END

NOTES ON PARTICIPATION

1. From the beginning of this speech, Toyman is talking directly to the audience, but collectively rather than to individuals (which could be uncomfortable for some children). He should pause briefly for answers to his questions, although it doesn't matter if, at first, they are slow to respond. This is an introduction to the whole play and his approach thus sets the tone for further participation. He should concentrate on character and his happy, excited mood. Avoid 'talking down' at any time. The members of the audience are his **friends** and equals.

2. The pom-pom-pom should be said at a brisk but not too fast pace. The rhythmical beat is the rythm of lively walking for Beauty, the doll. Toyman here, and later, can bring the audience voices to a stop by merely raising and slowing down his voice. There is no need to 'conduct' or 'ssh' the audience here or at any other time.

3. This second time the audience will need prompting.

4. They will say the words with Toyman without any 'rehearsal'.

5. They may tell her that he has gone for his book in which case she can ask what a "book" is, etc.

6. They will probably remind him about the book.

7. They may count with Toyman if he is not too fast. This, however, is not a deliberate intention and there is no need to work for it.

8. Someone may remember the date and repeat it for him, but there is no need to make it a memory test for the audience.

9. They may answer, but don't let it hold up the dialogue.

10. In most cases, the answer will be yes, but someone may know the actual number which will vary from audience to audience. Check in advance if uncertain of the number and adjust dialogue accordingly.

11. The audience will hum with Toyman until Mirrorman is through the mirror. There is no need to tell them to stop. It should be noted that Mirrorman 'hums' but thereafter it is referred to as 'the hum'.

12. The word "wish" may be repeated with intensity of feeling rather than volume - or it may be a silent wish. Sometimes, the latter is preferable because the audience may decide to 'wish' away the witch on her second entrance and this can cause some problems for the actor concerned. See note (18).

13. The hum may begin the instant Mirrorman puts his hands on the mirror, in which case cut the dialogue.

14. The audience may give the Plonk Ooooffff as soon as Beauty has said it in which case she should immediately stand and cut the remaining dialogue.

15. The old lady is, of course, the Witch; the audience may recognize her and some members may try to warn Mirrorman or Toyman; should this become very noticeable, one of them might acknowledge the warnings and possibly consult the others. In this case - and should participation become strong and insistent at any moment during this scene, the Witch should quickly find Toyman's book and exit - the dialogue accordingly being cut.

16. It is possible that the audience may tell Toyman she took his book as soon as he returns - in which case cut dialogue up to this point.

17. The 'poms' will stop as she gets to the box and the Oooofff Plonk will follow without further prompting.

18. It is possible that the Witch's arrival will produce excited calls and shouts for help. Alternatively the audience may decide to "wish" her away (see note 12). If either method becomes vociferously insistent, the Witch and Beauty must be prepared to cut the entire scene except the Witch must, before she exits, put the spell on Beauty by using a big gesture, thus stopping her from being able to move or talk.

19. It is possible, but rare, that some members of the audience may decide to tell the Witch where the book is in order to save Beauty. The Witch may ignore the audience altogether (which is wise), the assumption being that she doesn't hear or see them. Alternatively, a solution is to have Beauty try to stop them telling her by words and gestures until the Witch, in exasperation, puts a single spell on her to stop her talking and moving. Once the latter is done, even an Oooofff Plonk can't move her off the box which contains the book.

20. The audience may, of course, inform them that the Witch has been here the instant they come in, in which case Mirrorman and Toyman should immediately go to Beauty and discover that she cannot talk or move. They may also inform Toyman that his book is back...

21. Obtain general information and pick this up from many sources rather than expecting or allowing a long explanation from individuals. Mirrorman and Toyman should, in effect, communicate with half the audience each for only a short time. Generally information about the first two spells will quickly be given. The third may or may not be related; adjust dialogue accordingly.

22. The word "Listen!" spoken clearly and urgently will obtain silence.

23. Mirrorman should remain strongly efficient and in character during this sequence which is directly related to classroom drama. The urgency of this situation should result in 100% willingness to be involved so that all Mirrorman need do is observe to see what is happening with the whole audience, using his voice and the words as control factors. The words are written with particular care for sequence of action and built in control. Toyman should either sit quietly and observe or participate himself without too much emphasis. It is important that he does not give a "performance" which might cause the audience to watch or imitate him.

24. Select quickly and without hesitation from volunteers. Keep the urgency and "Magical" quality attached to the book.

25. It is most likely that no prompting will be needed (see note 12).

26. There is no need to insist on specific repetition of the words: that is, if Mirrorman concentrates himself on creating the mood and atmosphere, keeping the words long (use the vowel sounds) and slow. Toyman can pick them up and say them almost with him, as will the audience. The rhythm and repetition helps this.

27. While participation is not intended in this sequence and Mirrorman and Toyman should pay no attention to any audience involvement, the nature of the scene plus the rhythmic repetition of the words sometimes encourages spontaneous participation which can add to the dramatic atmosphere; it is very important, however, that the characters concentrate on building to an effective climax and do not allow themselves to be distracted by audience.

28. Sometimes the excitement engendered by the climax of the play may encourage comments or suggestions from the audience as to where the Witch might be. It is important that these should not be pursued (although the subject might provide interesting material for a follow-up session of creative drama after the play is over). Mirrorman should be firmly conclusive in his statement "She'll never come back" and Toyman should transfer attention back to Beauty in order that the play may proceed to a peaceful conclusion.

OTHER TITLES AVAILABLE FROM BAKER'S PLAYS

CANDIDA

George Bernard Shaw
Adapted and abridged by Aurand Harris

Comedy / 3m, 2f/ Interior

Probably Shaw's most popular play, *Candida* recounts the love sickness of young poet Eugene Marchbanks for Candida, wife of the Rev. Morell. At first, Morell is amused; but when he begins to doubt his wife's love, he becomes disturbed and angered. The poet becomes the stronger suitor, Morell realizes his weaknesses and Candida, one of the most remarkable women in dramatic literature, gives strength to her husband and teaches Marchbanks how to love. Harris offers a superb adaptation for competition, for study, and for introduction to one of the classics of modern theatre.

OTHER TITLES AVAILABLE FROM BAKER'S PLAYS

HIDE AND SHRIEK

Tim Kelly

Mystery Farce / 5m, 9f / Interior

June Hungerford is being hounded by Edwina Hyde, a dangerous young woman who is convinced June has stolen the man she loves. Desperate, June heads for the hills, where she encounters a bizarre hillbilly family. They take her in because she looks exactly like Daisy Belle, a relative who has disappeared. Daisy Belle gets a quarterly check from a law firm that always insists on seeing her in person. June agrees to impersonate Daisy Belle because she mistakenly believes she has murdered a man. Then there's the matter of sixty thousand dollars hidden somewhere. Finally Daisy Belle comes home and Edwina shows up. Watch what happens when two Daisy Belles and Edwina meet! And where did Daisy Belle hide that sixty thousand dollars? The over-the-top action, chills and thrills, and hysterically funny dialogue never stop!

"Outrageous silliness... you'll chuckle for a week."
– *Canyon Call*

www.ingramcontent.com/pod-product-compliance
Lightning Source LLC
Chambersburg PA
CBHW070422120726
47909CB00005B/1761